MEET THE GIRL TALK CHARACTERS

Sabrina Wells is petite, with curly auburn hair, sparkling hazel eyes, and a bubbly personality. Sabrina loves magazines, shopping, sleepovers, and most of all, she loves talking to her best friends.

Katie Campbell is a straight-A student and super athlete. With her blond hair, blue eyes, and matching clothes, she's everyone's idea of Little Miss Perfect. But Katie has a few surprises for everyone, including herself!

Randy Zak has just moved to Acorn Falls from New York City, and is she ever cool! With her radical spiked haircut and her hip New York clothes, Randy teaches everyone just how much fun it is to be different.

Allison Cloud is a Native American Indian. Allison's supersmart and really beautiful. But she has one major problem: She's thirteen years old, five foot seven, and still growing!

SABRINA WINS BIG!

By L. E. Blair

GIRL TALK® series created by Western Publishing Company, Inc.

Western Publishing Company, Inc., Racine, Wisconsin 53404

Text by Carol McCarren

Chapter One

"Does anybody have a pen?"

I didn't look up to see if anyone was listening. It was chaos here in the Wells residence — there must have been about ten kids sprawled out in the living room. I'm Sabrina Wells, by the way. It was almost four thirty-five on a Saturday afternoon and I was running out of time. I had less than half an hour to get my Totally Teen Fantasy Sweepstakes entry into the mail. It had to go out by five o'clock. That's the last time they pick up mail on Saturday in Acorn Falls. It's one of the drawbacks of living in a small town in Minnesota. If I mailed it on Sunday, my entry wouldn't be postmarked until Monday. And then I'd be disqualified.

"Does anyone have a black pen that works?" I called out, frantically shaking my ballpoint. "Mine's all out of ink."

"I'll get one," my friend Allison Cloud said,

looking up from the book she was reading.

"Check my dad's desk," I suggested.

I was really glad when Allison got up to help, because no one else was paying much attention to me. I guess it's because the Totally Teen Fantasy Sweepstakes is about the twentieth contest I've entered in the past six months. I guess nobody believes that a twelve-year-old girl could ever win a national sweepstakes. But I know I'll get a lucky break someday.

"Here's a blue one. There's no black," Al announced, throwing a new pen to me. Al's tall and thin, with long black hair. She was wearing a light blue skirt over a pink unitard, and it made her look like a ballet dancer. I'm short, with curly auburn hair, and my dad says I'm like a red tornado. Especially when I'm in a hurry. Which seems to be most of the time.

"Could you look in the kitchen?" I asked, giving the new pen a vigorous shake. "There might be a black one on the counter."

"Sabrina! You can't even find the counter," my friend Katie Campbell joked as she walked into the living room with a plate full of warm chocolate chip cookies. "It's covered with cookies!" she said with a laugh.

From the smell of things, I could believe that. Katie even *looked* like a cook. She was wearing a peach sweatshirt and gray leggings, but over them she had on a huge apron that had some telltale cookie smudges on it.

Of course, as soon as Katie announced that the cookies were done, everyone surrounded her to get some. In a second I couldn't even see her! It seemed like half the seventh grade was in our living room. Well . . . not exactly half. I do have a tendency to exaggerate. There were my three best friends, Allison Cloud, Randy Zak, and Katie Campbell. Plus my twin brother, Sam, and his best friends: Katie's stepbrother, Michel Beauvais; Nick Robbins; Jason McKee; Billy Dixon; and Arizonna Blake.

Once they had grabbed some cookies, everyone went back to what they were doing. Allison was reading a novel. Katie and Randy, who had been baking cookies, now settled in to eat them. Billy and Arizonna were listening to a new tape. Michel and Nick were looking at motorcycle magazines. Sam was playing a video game with Jason, and everyone was eating tons of cookies. But all I cared about was getting to the mailbox by five o'clock.

I was kneeling at the coffee table trying to get my entry form together. The Totally Teen Fantasy Sweepstakes is a big contest, so everything was taking twice as long as I thought it would. The contest bulletin was long, as usual. But I love reading contest bulletins because they put my name in big letters across the top. It makes me feel like a star. I know the contest bulletin is done by computer and that everyone gets the same one, but I still love reading it.

This one said: MISS SABRINA WELLS COULD SOON BE $5,000 RICHER! That was great. But the sentence I liked best read: MISS SABRINA WELLS HAS A ONE-IN-TEN CHANCE OF BECOMING A WINNER. A one-in-ten chance. That didn't sound too hard to me.

First I had to play the scratch-off cards to see if I was an instant winner.

"Hey, let me do some of those," Randy said. She knelt down next to me. "I love scratch-off contests. D used to buy me an Instant Win ticket every Wednesday back in New York." Randy always calls her mother M and her father D.

"Great," I said, handing her a few cards. "I need all the help I can get."

I watched Randy scratch off the cards with

her neon-orange fingernail. Randy's from New York City and she's really cool. She's always doing unusual things, like painting her spiky black hair or putting together some really rad new fashions. Today she was wearing a neon-orange jumpsuit that matched her polish exactly.

"No win here," Randy announced, uncovering the last card. But I didn't mind. The instant-winner prize was just a set of encyclopedias. I think encyclopedias are kind of a dorky prize. And we already have two sets, anyway. After that I had to attach a whole bunch of little prize stickers to the main entry form.

I held up a long sheet of stickers. "Want to do some of these?" I asked hopefully.

"No, thanks. Those take forever," Randy said. Then she got up and grabbed a cookie. "Good luck, Sabs. And don't forget who your friends are when you become a millionaire." She walked over to check out the tapes in the stereo cabinet.

Even though I knew she was just joking, my heart sank for a minute. It made me feel bad to think that my friends weren't taking me seriously. But then I thought about that sentence again. MISS SABRINA WELLS HAS A ONE-IN-TEN CHANCE . . . Just thinking about that one sentence convinced me that Randy was wrong to think I couldn't win.

But she was right about those stickers. Matching them up really did take forever. But finally I was done . . . with seven minutes to spare! All I had to do now was fill out the mailing envelope and find a postage stamp.

"Did anyone see a big pink envelope?" I asked, searching the coffee table. "It was here a minute ago!"

"You mean the contest envelope with the dollar signs all over it, and a bunch of writing on the front?" Sam asked without looking up from his video game.

"Yeah!" I replied.

"And it had a big rainbow on the back flap?" he continued.

"Yeah, that's the one!" I answered.

"Never saw it," Sam calmly replied.

"Sam! You're a pain!" I cried. I started frantically searching the cluttered table. "Stop teasing me. I'm running out of time!"

Even though we're twins, I don't think Sam and I are really alike. He's always teasing me. I mean, my other three brothers do that, too. But Sam really has a way of getting to me. Like today. I could tell by the look in his eyes that he had something up his sleeve. His eyes are hazel, just like mine. But when he's up to something, they get a funny twinkle in them.

Just then Sam sent the pink envelope sailing across the room like a Frisbee. "Take a chill pill, Sabs," he said with a grin.

I caught the envelope and began filling in my return address. I try to be really neat when I'm writing out contest forms. I always think it'll bring me good luck. But now my new pen was running out of ink, too! And I was running out of time! Panicking, I pressed down really hard. But just as I was about to put the last number on the zip code, a big blotch of blue ink leaked out and messed up all the numbers.

"Oh, nuts!" I mumbled.

"What happened?" Allison asked. She peered over my shoulder.

"My zip code's all blotched!" I threw my hands up in frustration.

"Oh . . . poor baby," Sam cooed as he ran over and grabbed the envelope. "Hey, guys! Sabrina's got a blotchy zip code!"

"Oh, no!" Jason cried, dramatically springing to his feet. "Think we should call an ambulance?"

Sam ran to the phone. "Code Blue!" he shouted into the receiver. "Ink Alert! Ink Alert! Blotchy zip code! Repeat . . . blotchy zip code! Call the paramedics!" Then he dropped the phone and started running around the room making siren noises and waving the envelope over his head.

Nick, Billy, and Jason ran behind him and started playing keep-away with my contest envelope.

"C'mon, guys. Cut it out!" I begged. The envelope flew over my head. "I'm not finished yet!"

Sam caught the envelope and leaped over the coffee table. "So, hire a secretary." He cackled. "You're gonna be rich! Remember?"

"Give it to me, Sam!" I yelled, trying to get up. But my feet were so numb, I couldn't feel them. I had been sitting on my heels for so long, I didn't realize my legs had fallen asleep!

"Sam Wells . . ." I cried, desperately trying to stand. But as soon as I got my balance, my feet started tingling and I fell right back down.

Now everyone was looking at me and cracking up. I knew my famous body blush was starting. I could feel myself turning red from the top of my head to the tips of my toes. I'm only four foot ten and three-quarter inches, so that doesn't take very long. I tried standing up again.

"Help!" I cried, wobbling down. I must have looked like a bright pink Easter egg.

I looked to Katie, Randy, and Al for help. But they were laughing so hard, they couldn't even move.

"Hey, cool it, dudes. Sabs needs help," Arizonna cut in, coming to my rescue.

Arizonna got behind me and lifted me up by slipping his hands under my arms. If I hadn't already been blushing, I sure would have started now. Arizonna's really cute. He's got long blond hair, and I've sort of had a crush on him since he moved to Acorn Falls from California. Just being in such a ridiculous position with him made my body blush even worse.

"Try stompin' your feet real hard. Like this," he said, stomping his own.

Sam began clapping to Arizonna's stomping. "Yeah, Sabs! Stomp your feet!" he shouted.

Then everyone started clapping and stomping and laughing even harder than before. Now I was really embarrassed. But the situation was so ridiculous, I couldn't keep from laughing. I felt like a giant Gumby doll as I flopped around stomping my feet. But I still couldn't feel anything.

"Whoa!" I cried, slipping farther down. Arizonna caught me under the armpits. "How romantic," I thought to myself, lying in his arms like a limp Raggedy Ann doll.

"Stomp, Sabs! Stomp!" everyone chanted as I pounded my numb feet on the floor. Finally they got back to normal and I stood up.

"Thanks, Zone," I said with a laugh.

"No sweat," he replied, smiling. My knees almost buckled again at the sight of that smile.

"Oh, wow! It's three minutes to five?!" I gasped, looking at the clock on our VCR. "I've got to get to the mailbox! Quick! Somebody find me a stamp!" I shouted.

I grabbed the contest envelope from Sam and started searching for a stamp. My mom always keeps a roll of stamps in the kitchen. But I couldn't find it anywhere. Now I was in a total panic.

Katie started fishing through her purse. "Don't worry, Sabs. I know I have one in here somewhere," she said.

"That's okay, Katie. I've got some right here," Sam announced, pulling something from his pocket. It was my mom's roll of stamps!

"Sam! You creep!" I yelled. "You knew I was looking for them, and you had them all the time!" I snatched them out of his hand. But the minute I did that, our dog, Cinnamon, galloped in and snatched the stamps from my hand with her teeth. Then she ran outside through her swinging doggy door. Cinnamon's a German shepherd–golden retriever mix, so she's really big — and really fast!

"Cinnamon! Come back here!" I yelled, grabbing my sweater and running out after her.

"Don't forget! You have to split the money with whoever gave you the stamp," Sam shouted after me as I started chasing Cinnamon down the block.

Sam Wells! Someday you're going to get what you deserve! I vowed to myself.

Chapter Two

One Thursday a few weeks later, I was sitting in Miss Munson's math class not really thinking about math. I was wondering why I still hadn't heard anything from the Totally Teen Fantasy Sweepstakes. Not that it was very unusual. After all, I'd never won a contest in my life, as Sam kept reminding me every time I checked the mailbox after school.

Of course, I wasn't totally sure I would win. But for some reason I felt unusually lucky. For one thing, I had been carrying around a bunch of good luck charms since I mailed in my entry form. You see, I forgot to kiss my envelope before I put it in the slot. I always do that for luck. But I had such a hard time trying to get Cinnamon's hair off the stamps, I totally forgot. So I felt I had to do something out of the ordinary, and I'd been carrying around my good luck charms ever since.

I was also thinking about a magazine article I'd read the night before. I have loads of magazines, and I try to read at least one self-improvement article a week. This one was called "Imaging Your Way to Success."

It said that if you really want something, you've got to be able to see yourself having the very thing you want. That's what they call "imaging." I guess it's sort of like daydreaming for a reason. Which definitely sounded good to me.

For instance, if I planned to win the Totally Teen Fantasy Sweepstakes, I was supposed to spend fifteen minutes a day seeing myself doing just that.

One of the things I couldn't see myself doing was listening to Miss Munson talk about probability for another second. So I decided it was a good time to try some imaging.

I figured that adding some good luck to my imaging session couldn't hurt, so I propped up my math book and quietly laid out my good luck charms. I had a rabbit's foot, a horseshoe charm, and a four-leaf clover. Well, it wasn't exactly a real four-leaf clover. Actually, I had found a three-leaf clover on a camping trip, and I had glued the fourth leaf on myself. But just having it made me feel lucky.

Hiding behind my math book, I closed my eyes and imagined what it would be like to win the $5,000 prize. I saw myself running to our mailbox after school. Then I pictured myself pulling out a large envelope with the word WINNER splashed across the front. I held it to my chest and hugged it.

I squeezed my rabbit's foot and took a deep breath. Then I imagined my parents and my brothers running up to congratulate me. "Sabrina! Sabrina!" They were laughing and shouting. Wow! This imaging stuff was really working! I could hear their voices loud and clear! I was getting more psyched by the second! "Yes! Yes! I won!" I blurted out.

Then I opened my eyes. There was Miss Munson's dragon-lady face right in front of mine. She was so close, our noses were practically touching! My heart was beating so fast, I thought it was going to jump right out of my body.

"Yes! Yes! Sabrina! You've won half an hour in detention!" Miss Munson announced. "Now pay attention, young lady!" She cackled like the Wicked Witch of the West. Then she slammed down my math book and marched back up to the blackboard.

I was glad that Miss Munson hadn't noticed my good luck charms. I quickly slid them off the desk and into my pocket. A couple of kids started giggling, so Miss Munson turned around, squinted her beady little eyes, and gritted her teeth. That shut them up fast.

Now the class was so quiet, you could hear a pin drop. I had the urge to look around, but I was so embarrassed, I just stared down at my desk. I knew my stupid body blush was coming on again. I could feel my cheeks getting red-hot, so I stuck my head in my math book and looked at the Laws of Probability. It turned out to be kind of interesting.

But by the time the class was over, I was totally depressed. According to Miss Munson, there's a greater chance of getting hit on the head by a meteor than of winning the lottery. I had no idea the odds for winning were that low. Suddenly my one-in-ten chance of winning the contest didn't seem too promising at all.

The rest of the day went downhill from there. We had pop quizzes in history and English. Then, to top it all off, I discovered I had left my gym socks at home. That meant I had to play volleyball in my sneakers with no socks, which was very uncomfortable. And as if that wasn't bad enough, as soon as the day was over, I had to watch my friends go off to Fitzie's Soda Shoppe without me.

My half hour in detention passed quickly, even though I had to write the sentence "I will pay attention in math and not daydream" over four hundred times! I tried to get the proctor to change it to ". . . and not practice imaging," but he didn't think that was a good idea.

Anyway, I hurried over to Fitzie's, and my friends were still there waiting for me. I could see Katie waving from one of the back booths as soon as I walked in the door. I started weaving my way to their booth.

"Have a good time in detention?" I heard a familiar voice snicker. Tinsel-mouthed Eva Malone was walking behind me. I turned my head to see her slithering into a booth next to Stacy Hansen. Of course, B. Z. Latimer and Laurel Spencer were there, too. They're all part of Stacy's clique, and they think they run the school just because Stacy's the principal's daughter. I was feeling pretty down, so I decided to ignore them. My day had been bad enough already.

Finally I reached Katie, Allison, and Randy and gratefully slid into their booth.

Katie gave me an encouraging pat on the back. "Don't let them get to you, Sabs," she said.

"They have raspberry frozen yogurt," Allison said brightly. "We know you like it, so we ordered one for you."

"Thanks," I said. My friends are the greatest!

"Cheer up, Sabrina," said Randy. "You don't have to look at Miss Munson's face for at least another twelve hours."

That made me smile, and we all had a good laugh over my math class fiasco. I had told them all about it during lunch. That's what I love about my friends. They always seem to know the right thing to say. Especially when I'm down. Which isn't very often.

"Have you heard anything about that contest you entered?" Al asked, sipping her root beer float.

"After what we learned in math today, I don't want to talk about it," I said.

"I hate probability," Katie commented,

spooning up a mouthful of vanilla ice cream.

"Me too," Randy agreed. She was eating an orange freeze. I was beginning to get very hungry. Luckily, Sally, our favorite waitress, brought me my raspberry frozen yogurt at exactly that moment.

"Actually, probability can come in handy in the right situation," Allison offered.

"But entering a contest with a million other people isn't exactly the right situation," Katie added.

Well, that wasn't really fair. "The letter did say I had a one-in-ten chance of winning," I pointed out.

"But you have to read the fine print on those things," Randy explained. "Like, did it say you have a one-in-ten chance of winning 'the' prize or 'a' prize?"

My heart sank when I thought about it.

"It said 'a' prize. Right?" Randy guessed. "Those dorky encyclopedias were 'a' prize. Face it, Sabrina. The odds are against you. Winning the Totally Teen Fantasy Sweepstakes is a total fantasy. It all depends on probability."

Just then there was a commotion over at the other side of the restaurant, where Stacy and her clique were sitting. Stacy was climbing up onto the table!

"Attention, everyone!" Stacy announced in a loud, clear voice.

"Oh, brother," I moaned, burying my head in my arms. For a minute there I thought she was going to say something about my having to go to detention. I know it sounds kind of paranoid, but I *am* kind of paranoid when it comes to Stacy Hansen. It wouldn't be the first time she was mean to me.

"Attention!" Stacy repeated as Fitzie's quieted down a little. "I have an important announcement to make."

"Are you going to buy ice-cream sundaes for everyone?" Jason shouted from the counter.

"Shut up, Jason," Stacy shot back. "This is important," she repeated, tossing her long blond hair over her shoulder and adjusting the fringe on her pink leather bolero jacket.

"If I'm not getting something for free, it's not important to me," Sam called out.

"Go, Sam!" Nick shouted.

"Everybody quiet down!" Eva demanded. "Stacy has an important announcement to make."

"Well, then, make it already!" Randy shouted at the top of her lungs.

"Okay," Stacy agreed, getting quieter. She pulled an index card from the pocket of her pink leather skirt. "Eva, B.Z., Laurel, and I will be holding a bake sale in the cafeteria at lunchtime tomorrow to raise money for the homeless families of Acorn Falls," she read directly from the card. "Remember, this is for charity . . . so please be generous."

Stacy looked around the room expecting a reaction. But everyone just went on with their conversations. I guess Stacy can't get over the fact that the whole world doesn't care about what she and her friends are doing. Not that we didn't care about the homeless people of Acorn Falls. But the whole thing just seemed too weird coming from Stacy Hansen.

Randy must have been reading my mind. "Man! What was that all about?" she asked. "They announced that during homeroom, too, remember?"

"Stacy Hansen! Raising money for the homeless!" Katie laughed. "That's a joke."

"If she sold her wardrobe, she could probably build *houses* for the homeless," I added. I was trying to be funny, but it didn't come out that way. Probably because it wasn't very far from the truth. Stacy's an only child and her family is pretty well off. Not that we're poor or anything like that. But Stacy always has the best of everything. My whole spring wardrobe probably didn't cost as much as the leather outfit she had on today.

"What do you think it's all about?" Katie wondered out loud. "Do you think she's changing?"

"That phony baloney? No way!" Randy scowled.

"She probably just wants to win the Citizenship Award," Al said.

"I never thought about that," I said.

Actually, I had forgotten all about the Citizenship Award. Every spring Mayor Miller gives it to a student who does something good for the community. They even have a little ceremony and everything.

"Yeah. Al's probably right," Katie agreed. "I can't imagine Stacy Hansen doing anything for anyone . . . unless there was something in it for her."

"Why does she have to raise money, anyway?" Randy questioned. "She could just give out her allowance!"

"That's for sure," Katie said. "When I was Laurel Spencer's skating partner, she told me that Stacy gets fifteen dollars a week!"

"Are you kidding?" Allison asked in amazement.

Randy was nodding. "I believe it," she said.

"Wow! Fifteen dollars a week!" I sighed. I'm not great at math, but when it comes to money or calories, I find it pretty easy to figure things out. "That's sixty dollars a month!"

"Awesome," Allison said, shaking her head in disbelief.

"Can you imagine what it would be like to be rich?" I sighed again, secretly thinking about the Totally Teen Fantasy Sweepstakes. "I mean really rich."

"Yeaaah," Randy said, swooning.

I nudged Katie. "So, Katie, tell us what it's like," I said.

"I don't know!" Katie shot back, sounding a little annoyed. "If you really want to know, you should ask Michel. He's been rich his whole life." Michel is Katie's new stepbrother. Her mom was a widow for a long time, and she recently married a rich man, Jean-Paul Beauvais. Katie still lives in Acorn Falls, but now she lives in a big mansion. She wasn't too happy about it at first, but now she likes it. We still tease her about it every once in a while.

"We're just kidding," Allison assured her. Al's really sensitive when it comes to other people's feelings.

"Al's right, Katie. We're just kidding. But tell us . . . what *is* it like to be rich?" Randy asked with a giggle.

Katie threw up her hands in surrender. "I told you. I don't know!" she said. "I still only get five dollars a week. My mom doesn't want to spoil us."

"Well, I'm certainly not spoiled," I cut in. "I only get four dollars."

"Me too," said Randy.

"Me too," Allison echoed. "And I have to do all sorts of chores and babysitting just to get that." Al's got a little brother named Charlie, who's really cute but a bit of a troublemaker, and a new baby sister named Barrett. And even though they have a live-in college student to help with Barrett, Al's still got a ton of responsibilities.

"Well, I know what I would do if I had

money," Randy said. "I'd buy a recording studio in midtown Manhattan, a condo in Greenwich Village . . . and I'd take taxis everywhere I went!" She smiled, obviously pleased with her decision.

"You'd go back to New York and leave us?" I asked, rubbing my eyes and pretending to cry.

"Well, I'd own a Learjet, too. That way I could visit on weekends," she assured us.

"Not me," Allison cut in. "If I had money, I'd spend it all on saving the environment," she said.

"*All* of it?" Randy gasped in disbelief.

"Well, most of it. I'd probably buy a lot of books, too," Allison added. "A-a-a-nd . . ."

". . . A ton of clothes?" Katie suggested.

"How did you know?" Allison asked happily. "But they'd all have to be made of natural fabrics, of course."

"Of course!" we all repeated in unison.

"I'd buy myself a hockey team," Katie said. "And a private skating rink, and then I'd buy . . ."

"A ton of clothes!" we all shouted together, laughing.

"Hey, what about you, Sabs?" Allison asked. "What would you get?"

"Hmmm," I said. "I'd have to think about that.

There are so many things."

There really were. First I'd buy the most expensive clothes I could find. Then I'd go around the world, first class. And then I'd buy a huge house.

That's the way they do it on that television program "Secrets of the Very Wealthy." I love that show. Every week they take the viewer on a tour of celebrity homes where the bathrooms are bigger than my bedroom. And that's pretty big, considering my bedroom takes up our whole attic.

I spent the rest of the time in Fitzie's just dreaming about how to spend lots of money.

Chapter Three

It was still so beautiful out when we left Fitzie's that I decided to take the long way home. Daylight savings had just started, so I still had almost an hour before dark. I love the beginning of spring. The days are warm, but the nights are still chilly. It's almost like having two seasons in one.

Taking the long way home took an extra fifteen minutes, but I figured it was a good way to get some exercise. I try to get a little bit of exercise every day.

According to an article I read in *Young Chic* magazine, a good walk is supposed to make you feel better. It also said you're supposed to think only pleasant thoughts while you walk. That's supposed to help clear your mind.

I decided to think about how great it would be if things could be perfect. Now, that was a pleasant thought. No Sam, bugging me all the time. No Stacy Hansen. No math homework. No Miss Munson. I was feeling better already.

Then I started thinking about winning the sweepstakes again. Even though it was just a dream, I couldn't help thinking about how awesome it would be to win $5,000. If I won that money, I'd be happy for the rest of my life. I just knew it.

I was thinking about all the things I could buy with $5,000 and how happy I'd be, when I suddenly tripped and dropped my books. At first I thought I had stumbled on a crack in the sidewalk. But it turned out to be the flap of a big cardboard refrigerator carton that was wedged in the doorway of an old building.

I looked around and noticed I was approaching the south side of Acorn Falls. I had been so busy daydreaming, I hadn't realized I'd walked so far. Not that it's a bad neighborhood or anything like that. But it's just not as nice as our side of town. It's kind of dirty, and the houses are smaller and all stuck together. Looking around, I noticed that a lot of stores were boarded up.

I bent down to pick up my books. Suddenly I noticed a woman and a young girl sitting inside the big cardboard box. The woman was about my mom's age. And the girl seemed to be around five years old. They looked like they could be mother and daughter. I was so shocked and frightened, I just stared at them. But when the woman hugged the girl closer to her, I could tell they were more scared than I was.

As I looked away, I noticed a beat-up old shopping cart nearby. There were two old suitcases, a couple of blankets, a few big plastic bags, some toys, and a bunch of empty soda cans in it. The minute the woman caught me looking at the cart, she reached up and wheeled it closer to her. Obviously I had stumbled onto one of the homeless families Stacy had been talking about at Fitzie's. With a sick feeling in the pit of my stomach, I turned around and quickly headed for home.

As soon as I reached our house, I decided to forget about the whole thing. After all, there really wasn't much I could do about it. But I couldn't get those people out of my mind. I was so upset that finding Sam in the kitchen stuffing brownies into his mouth actually cheered me up.

"Hi, Sabs," he said through a spray of brownie crumbs. "You rich yet?"

"Sam! You're disgusting!" I said, slamming my books down on the table. I didn't mean to be so violent, but he had been asking that question for two whole weeks! And I guess I was still upset from what I had seen on my walk home. Having Sam make wisecracks was the last thing I needed. Now I was in a bad mood all over again.

"My! Aren't we touchy today," my brother Mark commented. He had come into the kitchen just in time to hear my outburst.

Mark had a stack of mail in one hand, and he was dribbling his basketball with the other. Mark's a year older than Sam and me. He's only thirteen, but ever since he made the Bradley Junior High basketball team, he's been acting like he's in high school. He was looking at me intensely as he sat down at the table and popped a brownie into his mouth.

"Didn't check the mail today, did you, Sabs?" he asked.

He was right. I had been checking the mail every afternoon. But today I hadn't even bothered. I guess I had just about given up on the contest.

29

"What's the matter?" Mark asked, resting his chin on his basketball as he leafed through the envelopes. "Have you given up on being a millionaire?"

"Not interested," I said. "I just enter contests for fun. Don't you know anything about the Laws of Probability? You have a better chance of being hit on the head with a meteor than winning the lottery."

"That's what Miss Munson says," Sam chimed in. "And she should know. She looks like she's been hit by a meteor a couple of times already." I had to laugh at that. But Mark didn't even seem to hear it.

"Then you're not interested in going through the mail?" he asked, raising an eyebrow.

"Not interested," I assured him.

"Hmmm. What's this?" Mark mumbled. He picked up an envelope and held it up to the light. For a minute there my heart skipped a beat.

"Looks like an electric bill for Dad," he said, handing it over to Sam.

"Bill for Dad," Sam repeated as my heart sank.

Then Mark shuffled the envelopes and pulled out another one.

"Junk mail," he announced.

"Junk mail," Sam said, taking it from Mark and displaying it over his head. They looked like they were doing a magic act or something.

Mark pulled out a third envelope. "Bill," he announced.

"Bill," Sam repeated, taking it from Mark.

Now they were making me nervous. Even though I knew they were just kidding, suddenly I had an incredible urge to check those envelopes myself. But there was no way I was going to give them the satisfaction. Trying hard to keep cool, I turned around and headed for the living room.

"Oh! And here's one marked 'Urgent,'" Mark remarked casually. I spun around to look. So much for keeping my cool. "'Urgent, for Miss Sabrina Wells,'" he added, fanning himself with a large pink envelope. I just knew it had to be from the Totally Teen people. I could tell by the envelope.

"Let me see that!" I yelled.

Mark hid the envelope behind his back. "Thought you weren't interested," he remarked.

"Give it to me!" I cried.

Mark laughed. "No way," he said, getting

31

up from his chair. "You said you weren't interested." He was holding the envelope over his head with one hand and dribbling his basketball with the other.

"I lied!" I said. "Give it to me!"

"Make me," said Mark.

"It's my letter!" I shouted, trying to grab the envelope. "Cut it out, Mark."

"Yeah. Cut it out, Mark," my dad said. He came into the kitchen with my mom. They were both carrying groceries. "How many times do I have to tell you boys to stop teasing your sister?"

Perfect timing, I thought to myself. Boy, was I glad my parents were home.

"What's all the commotion about *now*?" my mom asked. She sounded annoyed. Which is no wonder, since she asks that question a hundred times a day.

"I got a letter marked 'Urgent,' and Mark won't let me read it," I said, taking the opportunity to grab it from him.

"It's just another one of those stupid contest letters," Mark said.

"So, why couldn't you just let her have it?" my dad asked, getting a glass of water. "Sabrina likes contests. Leave her alone."

My brother Luke came in from the living room. "Sabrina likes rejection," he said.

"I do not," I shot back. But I couldn't get involved in an argument. I was too busy tearing open the envelope.

Luke mussed my hair. "You do, too, squirt," he said.

Finally I got the envelope open. I unfolded the letter. Now I was kind of sorry I hadn't just taken the letter to my room and opened it there. It wasn't that I didn't want my family around if I won. But I sure was going to feel like a total dork if I didn't. Luckily, no one was paying much attention to me anymore. My mom and dad were busy with the groceries, and my piggo brothers were still downing brownies. Nervously I read the first line.

WINNER NOTIFICATION, it said in big green letters. It's probably a set of encyclopedias, I thought to myself, trying not to get excited. Calmly I read the second line. DEAR MISS WELLS, it said. CONGRATULATIONS! YOU ARE THE GRAND PRIZE WINNER OF OUR $5,000 TOTALLY TEEN FANTA-SY SWEEPSTAKES!

Not believing my eyes, I read it again. My

palms got sweaty and I could feel my heart beating a million miles a minute. I glanced through the rest of the letter to make sure I was reading what I thought I was reading. I couldn't believe it. It was official. An official notification letter.

"I won," I said quietly, staring at the letter.

"Yeah, right," Mark said. "What did you win? A magazine subscription?"

"No. I won the money," I whispered. I looked up at my family in amazement.

My mother came up behind me to peer over my shoulder. "Let me see that," she said. Slowly she read the entire letter.

"Well?" my father asked.

"She won the money," my mom confirmed. Mark spun around to look.

"She won?" Luke asked, his eyes widening in shock.

"She won?" Sam asked. He looked dumbfounded. He had even stopped eating his brownie.

"She won the money," my mom repeated. She looked a little dazed.

I beamed at my family. Their mouths were hanging open in shock.

"I did," I screamed, leaping into the air. "I won! I won!!!" I shouted, hugging my mom and running for the phone. "I won $5,000! I'm rich! I'm rich! I'm rich!"

Chapter Four

Sabrina calls Katie.

KATIE: Hello, Katie speaking.

SABRINA: Hi, Katie. It's Sabrina.

KATIE: Hi, Sabs. What's going on?

(Sabrina is breathless with excitement.)

SABRINA: Katie, you're not going to believe it! Not in a million years. You're never going to believe what just happened. I won!

KATIE: You won?

SABRINA: Can you believe it? I couldn't. I still don't. But I do . . . I did. I won $5,000!

KATIE: Whoa! Sabs, slow down. What *are* you talking about?

SABRINA: The Totally Teen Fantasy Sweepstakes. I won the Totally Teen Fantasy Sweepstakes!

(Katie screams.)

KATIE: Are you *kidding*?

SABRINA: No! I have the letter right here in my hand.

(Sabrina screams.)

KATIE: Are you sure?

SABRINA: I still can't believe it. But it's true. I'm rich!

KATIE: Sabs, that's totally awesome!

SABRINA: But promise you won't tell anyone.

KATIE: Not even Al or Randy?

SABRINA: Especially not Al or Randy. I want to do it myself. In person. I would've told you in person, but I couldn't wait. I just had to tell someone.

KATIE: I still can't believe it! What are you going to do with all that money?

(Sabrina laughs.)

SABRINA: Spend it!

KATIE: Wow! $5,000! What are you going to spend it on?

(Sabrina takes a deep breath.)

SABRINA: I'm not sure yet. I don't know where to start. But I can't talk about it now. I've got to read a whole bunch of stuff. There are

	forms to fill out and everything.
KATIE:	You mean, you don't have the money yet?
SABRINA:	No. My parents have to sign consent papers because I'm not an adult. The sooner they do that, the sooner I'll get my money.
KATIE:	Then you'd better get going. The sooner you get your money, the sooner you can spend it.
SABRINA:	But don't forget, Katie . . . this is our secret.
KATIE:	I won't tell. But it's going to kill me.
SABRINA:	If *I* can hold it in, *you* can hold it in. Promise?
KATIE:	Promise.
SABRINA:	See you tomorrow. Bye.
KATIE:	Bye.

Sabrina hangs up. Ten seconds later she dials Randy.

MRS. ZAK:	Hello.
SABRINA:	Oh, hi, Olivia. It's Sabrina. Is Randy there?
MRS. ZAK:	Sure, Sabrina. I'll get her for you.

(*Mrs. Zak calls Randy.*)

RANDY: Hey, Sabrina. What's up?

SABRINA: I beat the odds, Ran. And I didn't even get hit on the head with a meteor or anything!

RANDY: Huh?

SABRINA: I know you said the odds were against me . . . but I still won $5,000!

RANDY: Sure, Sabrina. I believe you. Tell me another one.

SABRINA: No. Seriously, Randy. I did. I won first prize in the Totally Teen Fantasy Sweepstakes.

RANDY: Who hit you on the head? Sam? You're hallucinating.

SABRINA: I'm psyched! I'm rich! But I'm definitely not hallucinating. Really, Ran! I won! I have the letter right here in my hand. It's real!

RANDY: Oh, man, Sabrina. You really mean it! Who else knows about this?

SABRINA: Nobody. Except my family. And Katie. And you. But you've got to promise me you won't tell anyone. Especially Al.

RANDY: Why not? This is so rad, I'm going to burst.

SABRINA: I want to tell her in person. I mean, I've just got to see her face when I tell her. It's just so awesome.

RANDY: What did Sam say?

SABRINA: He still hasn't closed his mouth. I think he's in shock.

RANDY: So am I.

SABRINA: Me too. I just keep pinching myself to make sure I'm not dreaming. My whole arm is black and blue.

RANDY: Wow! 5,000 buckeroos! And it's all yours! Unreal. What are you going to spend it on?

SABRINA: Clothes! Jewelry! Limousines! You name it.

RANDY: Can I help?

(*Sabrina giggles.*)

SABRINA: Spending money is one thing I'm sure I won't need help with. But you can watch.

RANDY: Thanks a lot.

SABRINA: I'm just kidding. I'll treat you to lunch on Saturday.

RANDY: What about tomorrow?

SABRINA: Okay. I'll treat you to lunch on Friday *and* Saturday. Okay?

RANDY: It's a start. But I'd prefer a little red Corvette.

SABRINA: I'll think about it. But I have to get going. And remember, not a word to Allison.

RANDY: Suppose she guesses.

SABRINA: Oh, right. Cut it out, Randy. Promise me you won't tell?

RANDY: I'll do anything for a little red Corvette.

(Sabrina laughs.)

RANDY: My lips are sealed. *Ciao.*

SABRINA: *Ciao.*

Sabrina hangs up. Ten seconds later she dials Allison.

ALLISON: Allison Cloud here.

SABRINA: Al. I just won $5,000!

ALLISON: Sabrina? Is that you?

SABRINA: Yeah, Al. It's me.

ALLISON: And you just won $5,000? You're putting me on.

SABRINA: No. Really, Allison. It's true. The letter came this afternoon. I really won first prize in the Totally Teen Fantasy Sweepstakes.

ALLISON: Are you sure this isn't another one of Sam's jokes?

SABRINA: Positive. My mom and dad even checked it out.

(*Allison is so stunned, she can't speak.*)

SABRINA: Al? Are you there?

ALLISON: I'm here. I'm just so . . .

SABRINA: Stunned? Amazed? Astonished?

ALLISON: Yes . . . but I'm . . . I'm really happy for you, Sabs. Wow! $5,000! That's a lot of . . . responsibility.

SABRINA: I think it's a lot of fun!

ALLISON: I'm sure it will be. But, you know, you'll probably have to pay taxes on it.

SABRINA: You think so? I don't. But who cares? I can afford it. I can afford anything. I'm rich!

ALLISON: Oh, come on, Sabrina. Your parents aren't going to let you spend all that money.

SABRINA: Why not? It's my money. I won it.

ALLISON: I know you won it. But they'll probably want you to save most of it. For college or something.

(*Sabrina is quiet.*)

SABRINA: That doesn't sound like very much fun.

ALLISON: Well, maybe they won't. But I'm sure they'll suggest you invest some of it.

SABRINA: Like in the stock market?

ALLISON: Oh, I don't think so. The stock market's too risky. I meant investing in something safe. Like C.D.s.

SABRINA: Is that good?

ALLISON: Very good. I was just reading about how C.D.s work. They can really give you a good return on your money if you don't touch them.

SABRINA: Sounds good. I'll look into it.

ALLISON: I'll bring in the article tomorrow.

SABRINA: Thanks! Look, I have to get going. I've got a lot to do.

ALLISON: Me too. See you at school. And congratulations!

Chapter Five

That night I was so excited, I didn't get any-thing done. I had a ton of homework, but I just couldn't concentrate. I tried reading the contest forms my mom and dad had to fill out, but they were full of big legal words. I couldn't under-stand any of it. My mom and dad didn't have time to look at the forms before they went to Mark's basketball game. But they promised to fill them out and get them in the mail by Saturday. According to the letter, my check would be sent overnight by Federal Express. That meant I'd definitely have my money by next week. I couldn't wait!

I tried to fall asleep, but I just kept tossing and turning. I couldn't stop thinking about how I would spend my money. I looked at the clock. It was 1 A.M. If I didn't get to sleep soon, I'd never wake up in time for school. Hoping some soft music would help, I turned on the radio.

When that didn't work, I tuned into CHAT Radio, the all-talk station. Luckily, "The Money Man Show" was on. They call him the Money Man because he's a financial adviser. I'd heard of him, but I never listened because I never had any money. Actually, the only thing I ever listen to on CHAT Radio is "The Diet Den Program." It gives you tips about nutrition and exercise. Once Randy and I called in and asked if potato chips were considered a nutritious vegetable. We thought it was pretty funny, but we never got on the air because the person screening the calls hung up on us.

Now that I had money, I thought it would be a good idea to hear "The Money Man Show." I listened for about ten minutes, but I couldn't understand what the Money Man was saying. He kept talking about rollovers, rates, and percentages. It sounded like a math class to me!

I was just about to turn it off when a woman called in and asked about C.D.s. I couldn't believe my ears! The Money Man said to do exactly what Allison had said: "Buy C.D.s and try not to touch them." He told the caller to buy as many as she could and just let them sit in the bank. That didn't make any sense to me. If I bought a bunch of compact discs, I'd certainly want to enjoy listening to them.

My oldest brother, Matt, is an electronics nut. He has a CD player in his dorm at college and he's always raving about how great the sound quality is. He says compact discs are "state-of-the-art" and a million times better than cassette tapes. Why anyone would let them sit in a bank was beyond me! I made a mental note to ask Al more about them.

Totally confused, I turned off the show and went downstairs. I hardly ever snack in the middle of the night unless I'm at a sleepover. But I was just so restless, I decided to have some popcorn and watch TV. I still wasn't the least bit sleepy. I guess all the excitement was really getting to me.

Even though we have a million channels on cable, I couldn't find anything I wanted to watch. The late-night talk shows were really boring, so I turned on the Home Shopping Mall. That's where you can buy almost anything right from your living room sofa. And it's on twenty-four hours a day. Tonight my favorite hostess, Rhonda Ray, was on. I always thought it would be really cool to be a Home Shopping Mall hostess. They have to describe all the items, and no matter what it is, they have to make it sound like it's the most exciting thing in the world. Since I'm a good actress, and I love to shop, I think it would be a perfect job for me.

After you pick an item you want to buy, all you have to do is call the toll-free number and place your order. Then they send it right to your door. But you only get a few minutes to call in. And if you don't dial in quickly enough, you miss out on buying the item. That's the fun part, because Rhonda Ray always makes it sound like missing the deal is the worst thing that could ever happen to you.

Once in a while I watch it with Katie, Al, and Randy. Sometimes Rhonda Ray talks to the callers on the air. We always crack up when the callers moan and groan about missing out on an item. First Rhonda Ray makes them feel awful, and then she's super, *super* cheery about it. Randy says it's all a put-on. But I don't think so.

Sometimes Sam watches it and dials in, just to see if he can get through on time. But he always hangs up as soon as the operator comes on. It's really cool.

I ate my popcorn and watched the Night Owl Sale. The first item up was an electric toothbrush. Rhonda Ray kept saying it was "an item no one could afford to be without." She kept talking about how important dental hygiene was. Which is true. But she made it sound like all your teeth would fall out if you didn't buy that toothbrush right away.

The next item was a home kitchen center. It was a combination food processor, vegetable peeler, and juicer. It cost $250 in the stores, but they were selling it for $99.99. Rhonda Ray kept saying how great it was for making low-calorie soups and desserts. The more she talked about it, the more I wanted it. After all, I'm always trying to eat healthy, and I certainly could afford it.

Impulsively, I dialed the toll-free number. But I didn't have to hang up when the operator came on. It was a little scary when she asked for my name and address. But it made me feel very grown-up.

In a matter of minutes I was an official Home Shopping Mall member. But I was really shocked when the operator mentioned the total cost would be $113.95! But then she explained that it included shipping and handling, plus tax. Since I didn't have a credit card, I had to order it C.O.D. That stands for Cash On Delivery. That meant I didn't have to pay anything until the package arrived. Luckily, that would take seven to ten days. I was sure to have my money by then.

I was just about to turn off the television and go to sleep when Rhonda Ray announced that a great deal on a CD player was coming up. And it came with twenty-five CDs! I didn't even listen to who the recording artists were, because I planned to put them in the bank, anyway. I couldn't believe my luck!

Now I was sure that winning the contest was an act of fate. If I invested in CDs, I'd make even more money! The more I thought about it, the more I was convinced that this was a sign I was destined to be a millionaire! I happily cuddled up with a blanket and waited for the CD player to come on.

Now that I had an official membership number, I could use the "Flutie" phone. That's a computerized phone that gets you through a lot faster than a live operator. All I'd have to do was press in my membership number. I couldn't wait to try it.

A half hour went by, and still no CD player. But there was a great deal on a radar detector. It was originally $149.00, but tonight it was selling for $79.50. At first I thought it was a dumb thing to buy, since I didn't have a car. But then I realized that I was only four years away from getting my license. I went ahead and ordered a detector. I figured I could always save it.

The Flutie phone was so much fun to use that by the time the CD player came on, I had bought an electric back scratcher, a folding picnic table, a decorative wooden bowl with carved wood fruit, and a toboggan. I knew I didn't really need all of it, but like Randy always says, "You gotta live large." And besides that, I certainly could afford it. It felt totally awesome to spend my money. I went to bed happy.

Of course, I was a little late getting to school Friday morning. By the time I reached my locker, Katie, Al, and Randy were already there waiting for me. Actually, it's Katie's locker, too. We've been partners since the beginning of the year.

I could tell by the way they were standing

there that they'd already discussed my big news. All three of them were posed with their hands on their hips, tapping their feet. I knew I was in big trouble.

"Don't forget, this is our secret," Katie teased.

Randy tried to imitate me on the phone. "Not a word to anyone," she said dramatically. "Especially Al."

Katie and Randy were slowly coming closer, reaching out as if to grab me. "I want to do it myself. In person," Katie said as she and Randy playfully lunged at me.

"I'm going to get you for this!" Randy said, pretending to strangle me.

"Not if I get to her first!" Katie cut in, shaking me by the shoulders, laughing hysterically.

Allison stepped in between us. "Hey! Break it up! Break it up!" she said as she pulled us apart. Obviously my friends had staged this in advance.

"Bravo!" I squeaked. I rubbed my throat, pretending to have lost my voice.

"Really, Sabs! Do you have any idea what last night was like?" Katie moaned as the warning bell sounded. "I couldn't sleep a wink!"

"I must have started to dial Allison fifty times," Randy began as I hurriedly opened my locker door.

"And I was dying to call Randy," Katie added. "But I promised Sabs I wouldn't tell."

"I didn't even know it was supposed to be a secret!" said Allison. "As soon as I hung up with Sabs, I called Randy. Then I tried to get Katie. . . ."

"And I made M tell her I wasn't home," Randy laughed.

"I did the same thing!" Katie said. "I just knew if I spoke to anyone, I'd spill the beans!"

"And I couldn't figure out why everyone was avoiding me!" Al exclaimed.

"Okay! Okay!" I laughed. "I'm sorry. I messed up. I just wanted to see your faces when I told you . . . but I was so excited I . . ."

". . . Just couldn't hold it in," the three of them sang in unison.

I managed to get my books out of the locker and slam the door, and then we all headed down the hall.

"Well, I tried," I wailed.

"Obviously Sam felt the same way," Randy commented. "He must've called every one of his friends last night."

"Forget about Sam. What about Mark?" Allison added. "The whole eighth grade knew by eight o'clock this morning."

"What?" I gasped.

"It's true," Randy said. "Between the two of them, the whole school knows by now!"

"C'mon. You're exaggerating," I said, trying to shrug it off. But the minute I said that, Mark came barreling down the hallway with a couple of his friends.

"Morning, Miss Moneybags," he said with a grin. Then he twirled his basketball on his finger and ran for the boys' gym.

His friend Brian was with him. "Hey, Mark," Brian shouted as the last bell sounded. "How does it feel to have a millionaire for a sister?"

I couldn't believe it. My friends were right. Obviously the word was out.

Chapter Six

The whole morning I felt like everyone was staring at me. Even kids I didn't know seemed to be seeking me out to say hello. But lots of them didn't even talk to me. They just sort of looked me over like I was a national monument or something. It felt kind of weird at first. But then I started to like it.

I began to feel very important, like winning the money made me a little bit better than everyone else. But the weirdest thing was the way Miss Munson smiled at me when I walked into math class. I think it was the first time I saw her teeth all year. And she didn't yell at me once the entire period. Obviously the rich get better treatment.

By the time homeroom rolled around, I was practically a celebrity. I nearly died when my homeroom teacher, Ms. Staats, asked for my autograph. Even though I knew she was just teasing me, it felt great to be so famous.

Katie started calling me "The V.I.P." That stands for Very Important Person. I certainly felt like one. Every time I turned a corner, someone came up to me. Ian Hooper, the president of the Music Club, mentioned how much the school needed new music stands. And Beth Cleary, the head of the cheerleading squad, reminded me that the girls could use new uniforms. Even Winslow Barton, the class brain, hinted that the Science Club was only $50 away from taking a fabulous field trip. Totally overwhelmed, I just told everyone I'd get back to them. Being so popular was really exhausting.

By the time we got to lunch, there were so many kids trying to get to me that I just ended up giving the whole cafeteria one big wave before I sat down. I felt like the Queen of England. But I figured that even the Queen has to take a break sometime. Plus, I was starving. Usually I just have yogurt and fruit for lunch. But today I decided to treat myself to some chili. Even our cafeteria makes that well.

"Wow. The V.I.P.'s splurging today," Katie commented as I dug into my chili. I guess it seemed kind of weird.

"Sabrina Wells can buy anything she wants," Randy commented. "She's rich, remember?"

Hearing Randy say that made me feel uncomfortable. And it wasn't what she said. It was the way she said it. I wanted to answer her, but I didn't know what to say.

Katie unwrapped the sandwich she'd brought from home. "So, how does it feel to be able to afford anything on the menu?"she asked playfully.

I hesitated. "It f-feels great!" I answered. The three of them were watching me eat.

All of a sudden I felt like I was sitting with three strangers instead of my three best friends. But then I figured it was just my imagination. Maybe Randy was waiting for me to buy her lunch or something. After all, I had mentioned it on the phone last night.

"Speaking of lunch," I announced, putting down my fork, "I'd like you all to be my guests at the Fortune Cookie tomorrow. And you can order anything you want!"

I really had no intention of saying that. I hadn't planned it. But sometimes my mouth works faster than my brain. The Fortune Cookie is a fancy Chinese restaurant at the Acorn Falls mall. We've peeked in the window a couple of times, but we always end up going to the coffee shop or Pauley's Pizza Parlor. Actually, it was no big deal. I could certainly afford it.

"The Fortune Cookie! Wow!" Al exclaimed. "You really mean it?"

"You bet," I assured her, starting to feel a little more comfortable. "And after lunch at the Fortune Cookie, I'm treating all of you to a fabulous shopping spree at Dare!" I went on, trying to sound like that British announcer from "Secrets of the Very Wealthy." Dare is my favorite clothing store.

"Awesome!" Katie squealed.

"Totally awesome!" Randy agreed. "Can we pick out whatever we want? 'Cause I've had my eye on these black leather pants that I'll never be able to afford."

"And I've wanted to get that green jacket that's been hanging in the window for weeks," Katie cut in.

"Oh, Sabs," said Allison. "There's this incredible pair of earrings I've just been dying for, but they haven't been on sale. . . ."

"Don't worry! It doesn't have to be on sale," I said. "You guys can buy whatever you want!"

I shouted. "And it's all on me!"

By this time, even I knew I was being a show-off. I was talking loud enough for everyone to hear. Even Stacy Hansen, who was trying her best *not* to hear me.

Randy held up her hands. "All right!" Randy said. "Give me high-fives."

"I can't wait!" Katie squealed with delight.

For a minute there I felt like I was going overboard. But I reminded myself that it really wasn't a problem. I'd get permission to borrow my mom's credit card, and I'd just pay her back when my money came in.

"This *is* really exciting!" Al exclaimed.

"A lot more exciting than Stacy's bake sale," Katie commented as we watched Stacy, Laurel, B.Z., and Eva trying to drum up business at the other end of the cafeteria. They were wearing matching aprons with HELP THE HOMELESS printed on them. But since my news was the talk of the school, nobody was paying much attention to them.

"Hey, Sabrina," Randy said. "Why don't you go over there and buy her out?"

"I wouldn't give her the satisfaction," I said, popping open a can of diet soda. "I hope her stupid bake sale is a total flop."

"Oh, Sabrina, don't be so mean," Allison jumped in. "Don't forget, the money's for the homeless. Not for Stacy."

She was right. I was getting a little carried away, thinking I was special just because I was rich. A picture of that homeless girl and her mother flashed through my mind and I winced. With everything that had happened in the past twenty-four hours, I'd totally forgotten about them.

Katie looked concerned. "Hey, Sabs. What's the matter?" she asked. "You look kind of pale."

"I'm sorry," I said, trying to erase the picture from my mind. "It's just that I can't stand talking about the homeless and that stupid Stacy Hansen. Still, maybe we *should* go over and buy some cookies or something. I'll treat."

"Of course you'll treat," said Randy. "You're rich. We're poor. You owe it to us."

That really bothered me, but I didn't say anything. I didn't owe anybody anything. It was my money.

We went and bought a bunch of cookies and brownies. Stacy was so busy ignoring me, I thought she'd fall over. The cookies made me feel better. At least I was doing some good with my money.

When we got back to our table, I told my friends all about my Home Shopping Mall spree. Except I didn't mention the radar detector. Now that I had had time to think about it, I realized it was a dumb thing to buy.

"Excellent. You're living large, Sabs," Randy said with an approving smile.

"I think the toboggan will be kind of fun," Allison said. "But what are you going to do with a wooden bowl of fruit?"

"Oh, I don't know," I said. I wished I hadn't mentioned it. "Rhonda Ray said it was a collector's item," I said, trying to make it sound like it was a smart thing to buy.

"Yeah. Lots of rich people collect dolls and coins and stuff like that," Katie cut in.

"But I never heard of anyone collecting wooden fruit," said Al.

Randy looked serious. "Too dangerous," she said. "Leaves splinters on your tongue."

"Give me a break," I pleaded. I was happy that things were feeling normal again.

"When will you get your CD player?" Katie

asked, taking a bite of a cookie.

"Yeah. That's a cool thing to have," Randy commented. "D promised to get me an awesome one next Christmas." Randy's parents are divorced. Her dad directs music videos in New York, so Randy gets the scoop on all the newest albums before they even come out.

"Speaking of CDs . . . I made you a copy of that article I was telling you about," Allison said. She dug into her bag and handed me a Xerox. "Except it's about investment C.D.s," she added with a giggle. "Not the other kind."

"You mean certificates of deposit," Katie clarified. "My stepfather bought me one when he married my mom. I've already made $18 in interest."

Now I was totally confused. Obviously there was more than one kind of CD. And I had bought twenty-five of the wrong kind! I wanted to ask questions, but after that "wooden fruit" conversation, I was too embarrassed. Luckily, Randy saved me the trouble.

"Well, I know everything there is to know about compact discs. But I don't really understand how those other kinds of C.D.s work," she said.

"It's sort of like a savings account," Al informed her. "For instance, if Sabrina bought a certificate of deposit for $1,000 and it earned 5 percent interest in a year, in twelve months it would be worth $1,050."

I did some fast calculations. "Because 5 percent of $1,000 is $50?" I asked.

"Right," Al said. "And the longer you leave a C.D. in the bank, the more interest it gains, and your money grows. That's why you shouldn't touch them."

Now I was beginning to understand. A certificate of deposit was just another way of saving money. I felt like a total dork. But at least I had learned something new. I folded Allison's article and put it in my pocket. Obviously there was a lot more to money than I had thought.

That night at dinner my brothers kept dropping these huge hints about all this stuff they needed but couldn't afford. For instance, Luke just got his license and bought a used car. It's really a bomb, but he loves it. He kept repeating how long it had taken him to save up the money, and how great it would look if he could just afford a new paint job. Then Mark mentioned how old and decrepit his basketball was getting. He kept talking about how he could probably score more points if he just had a new one to practice with. I couldn't believe how totally obvious they were being. I just ignored them and waited for Sam to put his two cents in. But just when I thought he was about to say something, my mom interrupted.

"Speaking of money . . ." she said. "Dad and I need to discuss some things with Sabrina tonight."

"Like how she's supposed to share her money with her poor, underprivileged brothers?" Mark asked.

"No way!" I shot back. "It's my money!"

"Sabrina! Don't be greedy," my dad scolded. He was obviously shocked at my reaction.

Even I was surprised at how nasty I sounded. It wasn't that I didn't want to share. But ever since I won that $5,000, I had the feeling that everyone was after a piece of it. First Randy, constantly reminding me of how rich I was. And now Luke and Mark! Part of me knew they were just joking. But another part of me was beginning to think they were serious.

I was even beginning to have second thoughts about taking my friends shopping.

After all, it sounded like they expected me to buy out the whole store. I was afraid that I wouldn't have anything left for myself. Maybe I *was* being greedy. But I didn't owe anybody anything. It was my money. I won it!

I was getting confused.

My mom pulled me out of my thoughts. "Sabrina," she said, "I think you should apologize to your brother. He was just teasing."

"I'm sorry," I said, staring down at my plate.

"Boy, what money does to some people," Luke mumbled under his breath.

Now I felt horrible. I kept waiting for Sam to make some kind of wisecrack, but he just sat there eating his chicken. Then Mark stuck his tongue out at me.

"That's enough!" my mom said. "As I was about to say," she continued, "your dad and I have some important matters to discuss with Sabrina . . . which means that you boys have to do the dishes."

"Aw, nuts!" Mark grumbled, giving me a dirty look.

"Not another word!" my mom warned.

Suddenly we all became very interested in what we were eating. And we finished the rest of our meal in silence.

Chapter Seven

Right after dinner my parents and I went into the den. I wasn't even asked to help clear the table, so I figured this was going to be a pretty serious conversation. As soon as my mom shut the door behind her, I was sure of it.

I took a seat in my dad's brown leather side chair. My dad sat down behind his desk. My mom sat on the couch across from me and pulled out a notepad scribbled with numbers.

"Did you get a chance to fill out the papers?" I asked.

"Yes, we did." My dad shuffled through the papers on his desk. "It took quite a while to sift through them," he told me. "First of all there's the matter of taxes."

Taxes! That's exactly what Allison had said. I should've known she knew what she was talking about.

"Why do I have to pay taxes?" I asked. "It's

my money."

"Don't say that," my mom pleaded. "Part of it is your money. But part of it has to go to the government."

I tried to remain positive. "Okay," I said. "I'll let them have . . . $30." I hoped that would be enough.

My dad laughed. "Sabrina, you can't decide how much tax to pay," he said. "The government tells you how much you owe them."

That was the last straw. Now I was angry. "I don't owe them anything," I said. "It's my money! The government didn't win the Totally Teen Fantasy Sweepstakes! I did! They didn't even help me fill out the contest forms or anything."

"Sorry, Sabrina. That's the way it goes," my dad said with a sigh. "Taxes are a part of life, and you have to pay them like everyone else."

"And this is really a wonderful opportunity to learn how they work," my mom added, seeing how upset I was.

I took a deep breath and sat back in my chair. I couldn't care less about how taxes worked. I just wished my parents would sign the consent forms so I could get my check and spend it. Hoping for the best, I tried to convince myself that paying taxes wouldn't be that bad. After all, I paid tax on clothing all the time, and that was only a couple of dollars. I decided to "think positive." But the news was a million times worse than I'd expected.

First of all, since I'm under fourteen, my $5,000 put me into the highest tax bracket. That meant I had to pay the government 31 percent!

"They call that a Kiddie Tax," my dad explained as I took a calculator off his desk to do the math. Thirty-one percent of $5,000 is $1,550!

"That's a pretty rude thing to do to a little kiddie," I commented, realizing I'd have less than $4,000 left.

"Then there's the state tax," my mom said.

I couldn't believe it. There was more! "State tax, too?" I asked.

"That's only 8 percent," my dad assured me, as if he were talking about eight cents. Nervously I put it into the calculator.

Eight percent of $5,000 was $400!

"But that leaves me with only $3,050!" I said.

"That's a lot of money for a twelve-year-old

girl," my dad reminded me.

"And we think it's a bit too much for a twelve-year-old girl to handle," my mom added.

I looked at her in disbelief. Then I looked at my dad, hoping he would disagree. I could tell by the look on his face that he didn't.

It just wasn't fair. It wasn't bad enough that the government was out to get me. Now my mom and dad were against me, too. I slumped down in my chair, totally defeated. "What do you want me to do?" I asked.

My mom came over and put her arm around me. "Sabrina, we know how tempting it is to just go out and spend it all," she said. "Anyone would feel the same way. But along with a lot of money comes a lot of responsibility."

"We'd like to see you put some of it in the bank," my dad said. He made it sound like a suggestion. But I knew it wasn't. I could tell by the tone of his voice that they had already made plans for my money.

"If you keep it in the bank, it will earn interest and grow," my mom said, trying to sound cheery. "You could use it for college."

Interest! Taxes! College! What ever happened to having fun? Suddenly, winning $5,000 didn't seem all that wonderful.

"So, do I have to put it *all* in the bank?" I asked.

"Not all of it," my mom assured me. "We've decided to let you keep $300."

"And you can spend it any way you want to," my dad added.

My mom and dad looked at me expectantly.

"Three hundred," I quietly repeated. That didn't sound like very much compared to $5,000.

"You can go on a wonderful shopping spree with $300," my mom said brightly.

As soon as she said the words "shopping spree," I got a sick feeling in the pit of my stomach. Little did they know that I had already been on one. My Home Shopping Mall trip was going to cost me a grand total of $468! I didn't even have my check yet — and I was already $168 in debt!

I didn't even hear the rest of my parents' conversation. I was too busy trying to figure out how I was going to pay a $468 bill with $300 and treat my friends at the same time.

Luckily, I remembered that the Home Shopping Mall has a money-back guarantee. As soon as my parents were finished, I called up and canceled my order.

It wasn't easy. First the operator said she'd never heard of anyone canceling before the order came in. Then she tried to convince me to at least see the merchandise before I made such a rash decision.

Not wanting to explain the whole story, I told her I had lost all my money in the stock market and could no longer afford such luxurious items. She was obviously confused, but she stopped bugging me. I got the feeling she figured out I was just a kid.

After I thought about it, I didn't know why I had felt I needed an electric back scratcher and a folding picnic table in the first place. I guess my brain had stopped working in the middle of the night or something. Actually, it was a relief to unload the radar detector and that decorative wooden bowl of fruit. But remembering what Allison had said, I decided to keep the toboggan. It would be a lot of fun. And it was a bargain at $58.

Now that I had only $242 left, I realized I'd

have to be a lot more discriminating when it came to spending. Since my money wouldn't come until next week, my parents agreed to advance me the $300 tomorrow. Then when my check arrived, they would pay the taxes, take their $300 back, and we'd discuss how we'd invest the rest. My mom said it all depended on the interest rates. I thought that sounded pretty fair.

Even though I wasn't very happy with the arrangement, I knew I had to accept it. After all, it's not like they were taking the money away from me. They just wanted me to be sensible about it. The more I thought about it, the more I realized they were probably right. But I still had tomorrow's lunch and shopping trip to worry about. I had to make $242 go a long way.

I decided I needed a budget. I wanted it to look neat, so I could see exactly where my money was going. I also wanted to be able to update it. I decided to use our computer. Even though my parents say that they bought it for the whole family, they won't allow Sam or me to use it without permission. I guess they figure we'll spend all our time playing video games or something. But since I knew my budget wouldn't take very long, I didn't ask permission.

Quietly I ducked into Luke's room, where the computer is kept. Luke had gone out to the movies with some friends, so I knew he wouldn't be home before eleven.

I turned it on and glanced through the menu. There, near the top, was a program called "Easy Budget." That sounded perfect. I take a computer class in school, so I knew exactly how to bring up the file. Luke had obviously used this program before, because all the blank spaces were filled in with numbers. I needed to get rid of them so I could put in my own.

I didn't know exactly how to do it, so I pushed F10. That's the HELP key. But it didn't explain anything, so I looked around for the computer manual. I spotted it on the bookshelf above me, but I couldn't reach it without standing on a chair. It's times like these that I hate being so short.

I pulled the chair over and stood on my tippy toes. Leaning all the way over, I could just grab it. But the book was a lot heavier than I thought and it fell on the keyboard with a thud. The computer started beeping and the numbers on the screen went wild!

Panicking, I lifted the manual off the key-board. But I must have hit the PRINT key by mistake, because the printer started running and the paper was spiraling all over the place like a wild roll of toilet tissue! I tried to turn it off, but when I leaned over to push the button, my hair got caught and jammed up the works. Now the printer was making funny noises and rolling up my hair!

Trying to save myself from an unscheduled haircut, I pulled the computer plug. The printer stopped rolling. I kept trying to untangle my hair, but it just didn't budge. Suddenly I heard footsteps coming up the stairs. Now I knew I was in big trouble.

"I've heard of using your head, but this is ridiculous," a familiar voice commented. Relieved, I looked up to find Sam standing in the doorway. He was laughing at me. I thanked my lucky stars it wasn't Luke or my parents.

"Sam! Help me. My hair's caught," I plead-ed.

"What'll I get for it?" he asked.

"Whatever you want!" I promised, tugging on my hair. "Just help me."

"All you have to do is push this lever," he informed me, doing just that. But instead of letting my hair loose, it just rolled it tighter. Now my nose was up against the roller and I could hardly breathe.

"Sam!!!" I exclaimed.

Sam was still laughing. "Ooops! Wrong lever," he said, pushing another one. As soon as he did that, the roller went the opposite way and I was free.

"Thanks," I said. Then I caught my reflection in the mirror. My head was full of static electricity and my hair was sticking out all over the place. I looked like something out of a monster movie.

"What the heck did you do?" asked Sam. "It looks like a cyclone hit this place!" He was right. There were miles of printer paper all over the place.

"Oh, Sam!" I wailed. "I think I'm in big trouble."

Sam looked down at the computer, suddenly serious. "So do I," he agreed. "You didn't ask permission to use this, did you?" he asked, toying with the keyboard.

I puffed out my cheeks and blew the air out

of my mouth. I always do that when I'm really nervous. "No," I said. "And I think I broke the printer and messed up Luke's files." I could feel myself starting to cry.

"Stop that, Sabrina," Sam said. "You know how to use a computer. We'll have this fixed up in no time!" Sam sat down in front of the computer and tried to turn on the disk drive. "Hey, why won't it go on?" he asked, visibly confused.

Silently I pointed to the computer plug sitting on the floor.

"You pulled the plug!" he shouted in horror. "Why did you do that?"

Anxiously I babbled the whole sad story. "And I think I may have lost Luke's budget program," I wailed when I was done.

"Boy, Sabs," Sam said with a sigh, putting the plug back in the outlet. "When you mess up, you mess up big time! Well . . . let's hope for the best."

Standing on my tiptoes to peer over his shoulder, I sighed with relief as the computer came on and the budget program appeared on the screen.

"Is this what you were looking for?" he asked expectantly.

"Yeah, that's it," I answered.

But then I turned pale as I realized that all of Luke's figures were gone.

"Oh, no!" I cried.

"What's wrong?" Sam asked. "Isn't this what you wanted?"

"Yes," I moaned. "But all of Luke's numbers are gone. That's what I was trying to do in the first place. But now I don't know where they went! How do I get them back, Sam?" I wailed.

"Sabrina, Sabrina, Sabrina," he sang, leafing through Luke's disk file. "You know how to do this," he said, pulling out a large floppy disk.

Luckily, Luke had made backups of all his files and Sam knew where they were. I easily copied Luke's program back onto the hard disk. Meanwhile Sam unjammed the printer and re-threaded the paper. By the time we were finished, there wasn't a trace of my disaster left.

"Thanks, Sam," I said. "I really owe you for this one." I half expected him to ask for $5,000.

"Aw, forget it," Sam said, going downstairs to watch television.

I was really surprised by Sam's reaction, but by this time I was too tired to figure it out. I gave up on my budget and went straight to bed.

Chapter Eight

When I got up Saturday morning, I decided to put aside $100 to spend on my friends and save the rest for myself. That left me with only $142. It wasn't exactly the budget I had in mind. But it was better than nothing.

I still couldn't get over how generous Sam had been the night before. I was so sure he was going to ask for money or something, but he never said a word. But then again, Sam's always surprising me. I never know what he's going to do next.

I had planned the shopping trip for the afternoon, because I had to wait for my dad to get the cash from his hardware store in the morning. I asked him if he could give me the whole $300 in quarters, hoping that my friends wouldn't notice how little it was. I wanted to make it look like as much money as possible.

My dad said he didn't think he could give

me $300 in quarters. But he promised to give me as many small bills as he could. I didn't know how I was going to tell my friends that my $5,000 was only $242. I had already promised them so much. Just thinking about the price tags at Dare made me realize that my $242 wouldn't go very far.

As I waited for my money to come, I picked out what I was going to wear. After trying on about five different outfits, I finally decided on my favorite acid-washed jeans and a white sweatshirt. I thought I should dress casually, since we planned to spend most of the afternoon trying on clothes.

Knowing I would need comfortable walking shoes, I spent a half hour searching for my special occasion sneakers. I call them that because they have tiny rhinestone studs on them, which I clean every time I wear them. I finally found them under one of my many stacks of magazines. I have piles of magazines all over my room. I keep saying that I'm going to organize them someday, but I never seem to find the time.

After I got dressed, I tied my hair back in a ponytail so I wouldn't have to fuss with it. I consider trying on clothes very serious business.

Just as I was finishing my hair, I heard my dad's car pull into the driveway. My heart fluttered as I realized that in a few seconds I would have my prize money. Well, some of it, anyway. My big moment was finally here. The night before, I had dreamed that my dad was climbing up the stairs carrying heavy burlap bags of loot with green dollar signs all over them. They were so heavy, he could hardly lift them. Maybe that's why I was so disappointed when I saw him climbing up the stairs with just one brown vinyl zippered pouch.

"Special delivery for Sabrina Wells!" my dad announced as he handed me the pouch.

Trying to hide my disappointment, I flashed a big smile.

"Have a good time," he said, giving me a big bear hug. "I've got to get back to work. See you tonight." He gave me one last grin and then turned and left.

Finally I was alone with my money. Trying to savor the moment, I sat on my bed and unzipped the pouch. Carefully I pulled out four stacks of one-dollar bills and two stacks of five-dollar bills. They each had white bands of paper around them marked $50. I ripped off the paper and fanned my fortune out on the bed.

I'd never seen so much money in one place. I had dreamed of this moment so many times. Anxiously I swept up an armful and hugged it to my chest. I took a deep breath, closed my eyes, and waited to feel something . . . but nothing happened. I didn't feel any different than I had a moment ago. I was kind of excited . . . and kind of happy. But it didn't feel as great as I thought it would.

At first I thought it was because it wasn't the full $5,000. But deep in my heart I knew that wasn't true. I was still trying to figure out what the problem was when Randy's voice interrupted my thoughts.

"Earth to Sabs! Earth to Sabs!" she called.

Startled, I turned around to find Randy, Katie, and Allison standing in the doorway.

"It's here! The money's here!" Katie squealed, making a beeline for the bed.

"Ah! The sweet smell of money!" Randy swooned. Then she grabbed a stack and fanned it under her nose.

Katie grabbed a bunch of bills and threw them up in the air. "Money! Money! Money! Money!" she sang.

"Are you sure it's all here?" Allison asked. She looked around at all the flying bills.

"It's all here," I said, mentally planning to get it back in the pouch before she had a chance to count it. "It's here!" I repeated. "And it's mine. All mine!" I hugged a great big armful and smiled as hard as I could. Now that my friends were here to share the moment, I felt a little more like I thought I would. But there was still something missing. Instead of being happy, I felt like I was just acting happy. Like my mind was happy, but my heart wasn't. Actually, I felt like a phony. But I decided to ignore my feelings.

"Well? What are we waiting for?" I shouted. "Let's get going!"

We gathered all the bills together and headed for the mall.

Our first stop was the Fortune Cookie. I couldn't believe how fancy the place was. There were elaborate Chinese lanterns on all the tables, and dozens of exotic plants hanging from the ceiling! But somehow I got the feeling that we didn't belong there. Maybe it was because the hostess gave us a weird look when we walked in with our jeans and sweatshirts. I guess she was wondering what four girls were doing there without an adult. When I noticed we had two waiters serving us, I knew I was in way over my head.

"This menu looks awesome," Katie exclaimed.

"I don't eat Chinese food that often," Allison said. "Someone will have to tell me what's good."

"Everything's good," Randy assured us. "Remember, I'm a Chinese food expert."

"Then I think we should let Randy order," Katie said.

I nervously scanned the prices on the menu. I didn't expect the Fortune Cookie to be as cheap as Fitzie's or Pauley's Pizza Parlor. But I never realized it was so expensive!

"Let's start with some appetizers," Randy suggested. Immediately my eyes darted to the appetizer section. "How about egg rolls and egg drop soup?" she asked, peering over her menu for our approval.

"If you say so," Allison said.

"Fine with me," Katie agreed.

Wow! One bowl of egg drop soup was $2, and the egg rolls were $1 apiece! That was $12 already, and we hadn't even ordered the main meal.

"That okay with you, Sabs?" Al questioned.

"Of course it is," Randy cut in before I had a chance to answer. "Sabs is rich! Remember?"

Hiding behind my menu, I took a deep breath. I wished Randy would stop saying that. It was really getting on my nerves.

"What's Moo Goo Gai Pan?" Katie asked.

"It's delicious!" Randy assured her.

Just then I found it on the menu. It was $11.50!

"I like shrimp," Allison said. "I think I'll be adventurous and try the house specialty."

I swallowed hard. Obviously no one else was looking at prices. The house specialty was $14.00! Panicking, I mentally began calculating the bill. It was already up to $37.50! And Randy and I hadn't even chosen yet! At this rate I'd have to cancel my toboggan. I hated having all this responsibility.

"What are you getting?" I hesitantly asked Randy.

"Lobster, of course," she said with a grin. "We're livin' large, aren't we, Sabs?"

The lobster was $17.50! Now I was beginning to wonder if she was getting the most expensive thing on the menu just to see if I would pay for it. Suddenly I felt like everyone was out to get me. I couldn't believe I had put myself in such an awkward position. Why did I have to be such a big shot in the first place? I could just hear my mother's voice saying, "Sabrina, don't count your chickens before they've hatched." She's always telling me that. But I never really understood what it meant. Until now.

"What are you having, Sabs?" Katie asked.

"White rice and tea," I said quietly.

I closed the menu and sat looking helplessly at my friends. I just couldn't stand it anymore. The pressure was too much. After all, I wasn't used to lying to my friends and being such a phony. But so many things had changed since I won that stupid money. First I had felt like I was better than everyone else. Then I got greedy. And now I was beginning to feel like I couldn't trust anyone. Not even my three best friends. No wonder they say "Money is the root of all evil."

Feeling totally foolish, I broke down and told them the truth.

Katie looked puzzled. "Gee, Sabs. You mean you've only got $242! Why didn't you just tell us that this morning?" she asked.

"Didn't you think we'd understand?" Al wanted to know.

"We're your best friends," Randy reminded me. She looked a little hurt.

Now I felt terrible about all the bad thoughts I'd been having. But after we talked it out, I began feeling like my old self again.

My friends all agreed that putting the money away was really the smartest thing to do. Then Randy suggested that we leave the Fortune Cookie and just split a pizza. But now I wanted to treat my friends more than ever, so we compromised and ordered combination plates. They were only $5.95 apiece, so the whole bill came to less than $30. I could certainly handle that.

After we left the restaurant, I wanted to buy them each a little gift, but they wouldn't hear of it.

"No. It's your money," Katie argued.

"She's right," Allison said sternly. "You put

a lot of work into winning it, so we'll just have to help you spend it on yourself."

"Yeah. We'll help you splurge on something really awesome," Randy said.

We headed straight for Dare and browsed around for nearly two hours. I must've tried on more than fifteen outfits, but I couldn't find anything I really wanted. I was so used to window shopping, I couldn't make a decision.

Just as I was about to give up, Randy broke away from us and ran to a display in the coat section.

"This is it." She gasped, pulling a light tan suede jacket from the rack.

"Ooooh. Feel this," Katie said, stroking her cheek against the finely tailored sleeve. "It's a genuine Nico DiPalma!" Nico DiPalma is a famous designer. All his clothes are pretty expensive, but they're really incredible.

"Now, that's a good jacket," Allison agreed, fingering the covered buttons. "And it's so light. It's perfect for spring."

Al was right. I had never seen a jacket quite like it. It was an unusually light shade of tan, and it had gold stitching on the cuffs and lapels. It was so soft, it felt like butter.

"I would die for this jacket," Randy said, swooning. "And it's not even black."

"The color looks fantastic with your hair," Katie said as I peeked at the price tag. "And it's such a classic style."

"But it's $180," I informed them, thinking of that phrase "A fool and his money are soon parted." I didn't know why all these corny old sayings were coming into my head, but suddenly they all made sense.

Allison took the jacket off the hanger and held it out to me. "Better to buy one good item than a bunch of useless junk," she said.

"Beats a decorative bowl of wooden fruit," Randy teased as she forced me to put it on.

"Sabs! It was made for you." Katie gasped. "You look awesome!"

Just hearing her say that made me think twice. And the jacket really did feel wonderful. Getting more excited by the second, I turned to the mirror and looked. My friends were right. It fit perfectly. And the color looked great with my auburn hair. I really didn't need another spring jacket, but this one was so special. It really made me feel rich!

"Get it!" Randy insisted.

"But it's $180," I repeated, not sure of what to do. I felt like I was on a TV game show or something.

"$180 is perfect!" Katie assured me. "You'll still have a couple of dollars left to get something else. Get it! You deserve it, Sabrina."

The more I thought about it, the more I was convinced that my friends were right. It was gorgeous. And I did deserve it!

"Okay!" I agreed, happily marching to the register. "I'll take it!"

They all cheered.

We all thought that counting out $180 in one-dollar bills was really funny. But the saleswoman and the people behind us didn't appreciate it very much. I couldn't get over how I had had so much money one minute, and the next minute it was gone. But at least I had a beautiful jacket to show for it. I loved it so much that I wore it out of the store, tags and all. I just wasn't ready to cut them off. I couldn't believe I had just bought a $180 jacket with my own money. I was so happy, I felt like celebrating.

Chapter Nine

"Let's all get ice cream. My treat!" I shouted.

"Great!" said Katie. "Let's go to the Candy Shoppe."

We headed over there and looked in. It was packed. The Candy Shoppe is the only place at the mall to get ice cream, so it's always super-crowded.

"Let's sit over there," Allison suggested, pointing to the only empty table.

"No," I said hesitantly. I was watching the waitresses running back and forth with trays full of sundaes. "I don't want to be sitting in an aisle seat with my jacket. Someone might spill something on it."

"Well, then, why don't you take it off?" Randy suggested, grabbing the table. "You could hang it over there." She pointed to the coatrack.

"No, I'm afraid someone might walk off with

it by mistake." I sighed, stroking the buttery tan sleeve. "I'll just keep it on."

"Okay," Katie said. "Maybe we should just order cones and eat them outside."

"That sounds good," I agreed.

We walked over to the take-out counter. I couldn't believe how long the line was. We were standing right behind a mother with a little boy eating candy. He was making me very nervous.

"What's wrong, Sabrina?" Katie asked, noticing how I kept stepping back to keep my distance. I must've looked like I was doing the Irish jig or something.

"That!" I answered, pointing to the little boy's big red lollipop. "I'm afraid he's going to get it on my jacket."

"Then maybe you should wait outside, and we'll bring you the cone," Allison suggested.

"That's a good idea," I agreed. "I'll meet you at the bench in front of the Ski Shop."

"Okay," Katie said. "But what flavor do you want?"

I looked up at the sign above me. There were over thirty flavors to choose from, but my decision totally depended on my jacket.

"How about chocolate–chocolate chip?" Randy suggested. "You love that."

"No," I said, not taking my eyes off the list. "I can't get anything brown," I informed her, indicating how light the suede was.

"Cherry vanilla?" Allison suggested.

"Too red," I said.

I read down the rest of the list. I couldn't believe it! I had owned my jacket for less than a half hour, and it was taking over my life! Plain old vanilla was the only flavor I felt safe with, but I really wasn't in the mood for it.

"I think I'll pass," I said, handing Katie a five-dollar bill. "You guys get what you want, and I'll wait for you outside."

Soon after my friends finished their cones, we realized it was time for Allison's father to pick us up. Our parents often take turns dropping us off and taking us home. As we headed for the parking lot, I was thinking about how well everything had worked out, when I noticed a drastic change in the weather. Early in the afternoon it had been warm and sunny. But now it was raining buckets!

I started panicking. "Al?" I asked. "Is your father going to pick us up where he always does?"

"Sure. Section 15, same as always," she answered, indicating the far end of the parking lot. "Oh!" She frowned, noticing the rain and remembering my jacket.

"I can't go out in that," I wailed. "My jacket will be ruined."

"Well, maybe you could put plastic bags over your shoulders and arms and make a run for it," Randy suggested.

"Are you kidding?" I asked. "I just spend $180 on a jacket and you want me to dress up in plastic bags?"

It sounded so ridiculous that we all burst out laughing. But we didn't have any umbrellas, so Allison ran to the car with half her sweatshirt pulled over her head. Then she had her father drive up to the door to get the rest of us. When we reached my house, her dad pulled his car into our attached garage so my jacket wouldn't get wet.

I couldn't believe how much extra work came with owning such an expensive item. Even though I loved it, I had to admit it was kind of a pain to take care of. As soon as I walked into the house, I modeled it for my family. Everyone agreed that it looked absolutely fabulous. Even Sam! I couldn't bear to put it in the closet because I was afraid it would get wrinkled. My mom said I'd have to put it away eventually. But she agreed to let me hang it in the living room for the evening.

After dinner we all sat down to watch TV. We try to make Saturday night "family night" whenever we can. I polished my nails, had a pillow fight with Sam and Mark, and then we all made ice-cream sundaes. I was certainly glad we had chocolate–chocolate chip in the house, because now I was dying for it.

Finally I felt like things were really back to normal. I was so glad I didn't have to worry about that silly money anymore. I was just thinking about what a relief it was, when the the ten o'clock local news came on.

I couldn't believe my ears when the anchorwoman announced their feature story: "Homelessness in Acorn Falls hits an all-time high."

My eyes were glued to the set as scenes of South Acorn Falls flashed across the screen. They showed the exact block where I had been last Thursday. Not wanting to get upset all over again, I started to switch channels. But just as I was about to, the reporter began interviewing the same woman I had seen that day. I couldn't believe it.

I listened closely as she described how her family's apartment building had burned down. They didn't have enough insurance to cover everything, and now they had no place to live. Then the camera panned back and showed the rest of her family. Besides her little daughter, she had a husband and two teenage boys. Her husband talked about how impossible it was to get a job when you didn't have an address.

Then the anchorwoman mentioned that there were ten other families in the same situation. Gulping hard, I looked at my family sitting around me in our nice comfortable living room. Then I looked at my new suede jacket. Suddenly all the confusion I had had about money became totally clear. Now I knew exactly what I wanted to do.

As soon as the news was over, I called the Home Shopping Mall and canceled the toboggan. I also promised myself to never, ever watch that show again. It was just too tempting. After that I went to my room and did a little thinking. I knew now that there were more important things I could do with my money than spend it on myself. After making a couple of important decisions, I went downstairs and told my family that I wanted to have a special meeting tomorrow afternoon to make an announcement. Then I called Katie, Al, and Randy and invited them to come, too. Just thinking about what I was going to do made me feel terrific.

The next morning I put on my yellow-and-white-striped T-shirt and my white jeans. Then I combed my hair back and finished off the look with a yellow headband and my white cardigan sweater. It was from last season, but it still looked brand-new.

Taking a deep breath, I carefully removed my Nico DiPalma jacket from its hanger, folded it, and put it into a shopping bag. Now I was sure glad I hadn't removed the tags. Since my parents were out having brunch with friends, I asked Luke for a lift to the mall. He was going to the Record Stop, anyway, so he said he'd drive me home, too.

As soon as I got to the mall, I headed straight for Dare. I usually hate returning stuff. But I was doing so much of it lately, it was getting easier all the time. Placing my bag on the counter, I told the saleswoman I wanted to return the jacket. Judging from the look she gave me, I thought she was going to say I couldn't. But when she asked me if I wanted my money back in one-dollar bills, I realized she was the same saleswoman who had sold it to me.

She made out the credit slip and gave me my money back. As I was leaving the store, I looked back and watched her hang my Nico DiPalma back on the display rack. It made me a little sad. I had taken such good care of it, I almost felt like I was saying good-bye to a pet instead of a jacket. But deep in my heart I knew that giving it up was going to make me a lot happier in the long run. Eagerly I went home and got ready for my meeting.

First I made a big pitcher of iced tea. Then I set the dining room table with my mom's special pink glasses and put out a small tray of cookies. A stack of white cocktail napkins, and I was ready.

I usually like to make a grand entrance. But I was so eager to get things going, I seated myself at the head of the table and waited for my guests. Katie and Al were the first to arrive.

"Where's Randy?" I asked.

"My dad offered her a ride —" Al began.

"But M was heading in this direction, anyway," Randy said, breezing in and taking a seat. "What's up, Sabs?"

Sam slid into the dining room like he was sliding into first base. "Yeah. What's the big news?" he asked. "This gonna take long?"

"Don't tell me you won another contest?" Mark grumbled. He and Luke stood in the doorway.

My parents nudged them into the room, and everybody took seats around the table.

"I hope it's not a new contest," my dad said. "I just finished signing the papers for the last one!"

"Don't worry, Dad. That's not it," I assured him.

"I know what it is," Sam said. "It was all a mistake, and they want you to give back the money. Right?"

"Well . . . sort of," I said. Then I had to smile because everyone was looking at me with such amazement.

"It's not that I have to give the money back,"

I continued. "It's just that I've decided to give some of it away."

Now everyone was staring at me, hanging on to my next word. Feeling happy, I told my family and friends about my new plan for the remaining $268.

My friends were shocked to learn that I had returned the tan suede jacket. But they cheered up when I announced that I was going to spend $100 throwing a superspecial spring barbecue for my superspecial family and friends.

Then I told everyone how I had stumbled across that homeless family they had shown on the news. I think it was the first time my brothers ever listened to me without making any wisecracks. My parents beamed with pride when I announced that I was donating $150 to the Homeless Families Charity Fund. My dad applauded, and my mom got up and gave me a big hug.

It was a little embarrassing, but it felt great. If anyone noticed that I still had some money left, they didn't mention it. Which was fine with me, because I still had one more surprise in store. But I was saving that for next Saturday's barbecue.

I spent the whole week getting ready for it. I love throwing parties. And it was really nice to have enough money to do it the way I wanted to.

I decided to have it in Acorn Falls Park so I'd have plenty of picnic tables and barbecue pits. I thought it would also be nice to have it near the duck pond. It's so pretty in the spring. After I decided where it was going to be, I started working on a theme. I always like to have a theme — it makes it a lot easier to pick the colors of the plates and decorations.

First I thought everything should be green, because green is the color of money. But then I realized that I wasn't throwing this barbecue just because I won the money. I had a ton of ideas floating around in my head, but one thought kept coming back to me over and over again. As long as I had been trying to keep all the money for myself, I'd been totally miserable. But as soon as I decided to share it, I was happy.

Even though it sounded kind of corny, I decided that the theme for my barbecue would be "A Happy Heart." I knew it was just perfect, because I realized that winning $5,000 didn't make me half as happy as having my friends and family to share it with me. After I figured that one out, everything else fell into place.

I bought red plastic tablecloths and pink plates, cups, and napkins. I also asked all my guests to wear something red. I got the idea from this article I read about planning an L.A. party. They always do stuff like that in California. For the centerpieces, I painted a couple of old Easter baskets pink and tied red heart balloons to the handles. I planned to put one in the middle of each table and fill it up with corn bread. My mom helped me plan the menu. She suggested that we make it a country barbecue, so we settled on barbecued chicken, potato salad, corn on the cob, red fruit punch, and apple pie. I just couldn't wait for the weekend to come!

Chapter Ten

Luckily, Saturday was a bright, sunny day. I left for the park extra early to set things up. I wanted to do it all by myself, but my mom said it was too much to handle. I knew she was right, so I agreed to let Luke and my dad come along to carry the heavy stuff.

As soon as we got to the park, I put on one of my dad's old shirts over my clothing so I wouldn't ruin my outfit. I wore my red-and-white-checkered blouse with my black jeans, pink socks, and white sneakers. Also, I'd found a pink ponytail holder in the shape of a heart, which was perfect.

I chose a table to keep all my extra supplies on, like napkins and cups and plates. I think it's important to be organized. By the time I finished setting up, it looked more like a Valentine's Day party than a barbecue! I knew I was going to get a lot of wisecracks and questions about my choice of decorations. But I decided I'd figure out what to say when the time came. In any case, I thought the tables looked great.

Before I knew it, it was noon and my guests were starting to arrive. I couldn't believe it when Katie, Allison, and Randy showed up in matching outfits. They were all wearing jeans, denim jackets, red cotton T-shirts, pink sneakers, and red hanging earrings. I could tell that Randy had picked out the earrings. They were big glittery balls and really wild.

"You all look awesome," I said, laughing, as they walked toward me arm in arm.

"This whole setup looks awesome," Randy said. "Nobody told me I missed Valentine's Day," she added with a laugh.

"It's just my way of saying I love you guys," I replied. I tried to sound casual, but I'm not sure it came out that way. I felt a little embarrassed for a second. But then, when we all giggled and hugged each other, I was glad I had said it. I think that sometimes you have to be a little daring when it comes to telling people how much you care. Obviously the rest of my friends were really looking forward to coming, because everyone arrived right on time! Michel, Arizonna, Billy, Jason, and Scottie Silver all came in the same car. And Sam and Nick rode their bicycles over.

As soon as Sam showed up, he took out his mitt and bat and got a softball game going.

"Hey! Let's play the boys against the girls," Katie suggested as we all ran to an open field.

The game lasted for over an hour, and the girls won! All the guys kept saying they let us win, but it wasn't true. Randy hit two home runs. And Katie hit four! She's really great at sports.

After that we were all starving, so we ate and hung out a little. I started feeding the ducks. But as soon as I threw out the first crust of bread, about twenty-five of them waddled out of the pond and practically took over our picnic site! They were climbing up on the picnic tables and trying to eat our apple pies! Finally we had to run after them and *quack* them back into the water.

After dessert my mom suggested we have a relay race. But we didn't have any batons, so Sam got the bright idea of using barbecued chicken legs instead. It was supermessy, but it sure was a lot of fun!

Then we had the greatest three-legged race. I guess Billy and Allison won that one because they're so tall.

I couldn't believe what a ball everyone was having. Every time I thought that things were about to quiet down, one of my friends or one of my brothers came up with something else to do. Randy brought her boom box, and we spent a lot of time dancing. Then Mark started lip-synching to some rap music, and we ended up having an unscheduled talent contest. Jason won first prize with his imitation of Miss Munson as an army drill sergeant. It was really a riot. Even my parents were laughing, because they'd had Miss Munson when they were kids.

I couldn't wait to see what Sam was going to do. But I couldn't find him anywhere. Right after the talent contest, there was a quick shower. But luckily, the park has a covered bridge. We all waited out the rain underneath it, and I led everyone in a sing-along until the shower was over.

After that everything was kind of wet. I was sure we would all head for home. But Luke took a huge rope out of his car, and we ended up having a tug-of-war in the mud! This time, the boys' team won. But it wasn't really fair, because they had Luke and my dad on their side. Since I'm the shortest girl, I was in the front and ended up with mud all over me! Between the rain, the barbecue sauce, and the mud, I was a mess. But I was having such a ball, I didn't even mind. My barbecue was a big success, and it kept getting better and better.

I almost died when my dad pulled a couple of cartons of eggs out of the cooler and suggested we have an egg toss. He had obviously planned it, which really surprised me. It's not exactly his style. I couldn't believe how involved he got in lining us all up and showing us the best way to toss and catch.

"Now, you have to be really quiet and concentrate," he said.

He and my mom showed us how to do it. I was amazed at how good they were. I couldn't imagine where they learned to toss eggs like that. It made me wonder what they did for fun when they were dating!

We all started tossing the eggs back and forth. My parents were the best. They went for almost five minutes without dropping the egg once. But then my dad went over to my mom and pretended he was going to slime her. He held the egg high above her head and kept making funny faces. It was really weird to see my parents clowning around like that.

"Drop it! Drop it!" we all chanted as my mom covered her eyes with her hands, waiting for the egg to fall. When she couldn't stand the suspense any longer, she let out a loud scream and started running. Then my dad chased her around the lake, and we all started doing the same thing. None of us were actually throwing eggs, but you just knew we were all waiting for the first one to break accidentally on purpose. As soon as Randy broke the first one, that was the beginning of the end. Suddenly there were eggs dropping all over the place!

We were getting so rowdy that a crowd of people stopped to watch. So much for a quiet egg toss! Everybody was running around having a ball! I couldn't have planned a better grand finale!

"Have you seen my brother?" I asked Katie, looking around for Sam.

"Come to think of it," she answered, "I haven't seen Sam in a while."

If I could just find him, it would be the perfect ending to a perfect day! Here I was, already a mess, with a raw egg in my hand, in a crowd of people. What an opportunity to get back at Sam for all the dirty tricks he'd played on me! After all, how many chances would I have to throw an egg at him and not have my parents yell at me? Carefully holding my egg, I searched the crowd, looking for him.

I finally spotted him on the sidelines, talking to a large bald man in a blue suit. The man looked kind of familiar, but I couldn't figure out where I knew him from. It was really strange.

I couldn't believe Sam was sitting out an egg fight! Usually he lives for this kind of stuff. But I didn't have time to figure things out right then. All I cared about was sliming Sam with my egg. Slowly I approached him. The closer I got, the more I realized that he was too involved in his conversation to notice me. This was going to be easy! Winding up my arm like a baseball pitcher, I swung the egg and let it fly out of my hand. But instead of landing on Sam, it landed right on the bald man's nose!

"Oh, no!" I gasped, cupping my hand over

my mouth. Suddenly everything came to a dead halt as the man squinted his eyes and reached in his pocket for his glasses. Obviously he wanted to search for the person that had slimed him. The crowd looked so shocked, I couldn't figure out what was going on. I got the feeling that everyone was in on a big secret I knew nothing about.

But the moment the man put on his glasses, I realized who he was. Suddenly I felt faint. I had just slimed Mayor Miller! But I couldn't imagine what the mayor of Acorn Falls was doing at my barbecue. And why was he talking to Sam?

"Nice going, Sabrina," Sam said, obviously embarrassed.

"This is Sabrina?" the mayor asked. He had yellow yolk dripping off his nose. "This is Sabrina Wells?"

"Yeah. That's her," Sam assured him, looking totally disappointed.

Now everyone was watching me, as if they were waiting for me to do something.

"I'm . . .I'm sorry, Your Honor," I sputtered, taking a bow, as if he were a king. I felt like such an idiot. Here I was, wet, muddy, and smelling like barbecue sauce, bowing to the mayor I had just slimed! But I was so confused. How did Mayor Miller know who I was? And what was he doing talking to my brother Sam?

"What's going on?" I asked, hopelessly bewildered.

Sam answered me. "When you decided to donate your prize money to the homeless, I called the mayor's office and nominated you for the Citizenship Award," he explained.

"And our committee selected you as the winner," Mayor Miller said with a smile. He fumbled for something in his breast pocket. "And since all your friends and family were going to be here today, Sam thought this would be the perfect place to present your award," he continued. "Except, at the rate we're going, I think I should be awarding you an omelet rather than this." He chuckled, pulling the award from his pocket. It was a small gold medallion hanging on a long red-and-white ribbon.

"Sabrina Wells, on behalf of all the homeless families of Acorn Falls, we thank you for your kindness and generosity," Mayor Miller said. Then he smiled and slipped the ribbon over my head.

"Thank you," I said. "I'm thrilled. I just can't believe it. . . ." Everyone whistled and applauded. I felt like I had just taken first place at the Summer Olympics!

Totally stunned, I stared at the medal and then looked at Sam.

"I can't believe you did this," I said.

"He sure did," Katie confirmed, grinning.

"You knew?" I asked, totally shocked.

"We sure did," Randy said with a smile. "But when we're asked to keep a secret, we keep a secret." Allison, Katie, and I all laughed with her.

"Well, you're not the only ones with a secret," I said, running over to my picnic table of supplies. Reaching underneath it, I pulled out a gift-wrapped package and handed it to Sam.

He was caught totally off guard. "What's this?" he asked.

"Open it," I said.

"If you say so," he said, tearing into it.

"Wow! A deluxe baseball mitt!" he shouted. "But how did you know I wanted one?"

"Sometimes twins can read each other's minds," I said, giving him a hug. I could've told him that I had asked Nick what he wanted, but I didn't bother. Just looking at his happy face made me feel like a million bucks.

"I can't believe you bought this for me," Sam said with a smile. "How much money do you have left, anyway?" he asked, eagerly trying on the mitt.

"It doesn't matter," I replied, looking at the smiling faces around me. "There are some things that money can't buy!"

Don't Miss
GIRL TALK #41
RANDY AND THE GREAT CANOE RACE

"Cookies!" Sam yelled. "Get 'em, boys, before Blabs and her friends scarf them all up!"

"We saw those cookies first," Sabs complained to her brother.

"Hey, it's the law of the jungle," Sam said. "Only the strong survive."

"More like 'only the greedy,'" Katie shot back.

"Look, we're men," said Greg Loggins, who's one of Sam's friends. He shrugged. "We need more food than you girls."

"Men? You'll be men in about ten years — maybe!" I said.

"Very funny," Greg said. He gave me a dirty look, then gulped down a chunk of cookie dripping with chocolate. "But while you girls were sitting around here painting your toenails, or whatever it is you do, *we* were out on the river with my dad canoeing." He rolled up his sleeve and flexed his right arm to show off his muscles. "You need a lot of food to build this kind of power."

He struck a pose like a bodybuilder, and Greg, Jason and Nick followed suit, grunting and flexing their muscles like a bunch of miniature Arnold Schwarzeneggers.

"I don't need to be a he-man," I said. "I can be a she-woman!"

But the guys just laughed as they headed off, still doing their exaggerated bodybuilder moves.

"You think you guys are so tough?" I called. "How about a little contest?" It wasn't exactly like I *meant* to say it. It just popped out. I can't always rely on my mouth to behave.

The guys all stopped dead in their tracks. "Excuse me," Greg said, spinning around. "Did you just say something about a contest?"

"She probably just blurted it out without thinking. You know how silly girls are," Sam said.

How could I ignore that? "You think you guys are so tough?" I cried. "Fine. We challenge you to ... to a canoe race!"

Out of the corner of my eye, I could see Al looking at me with a mixture of shock and horror. Sabs was standing off to one side, shaking her head and silently mouthing the word *no*. But it was a little late to back down now.

TALK BACK!
TELL US WHAT YOU THINK ABOUT GIRL TALK BOOKS

Name _____

Address _____

City _____ State _____ Zip_____

Birthday _____ Mo._____ Year _____

Telephone Number (___)_____

1) Did you like this GIRL TALK book?

Check one: YES_____ NO_____

2) Would you buy another GIRL TALK book?

Check one: YES_____ NO_____

If you like GIRL TALK books, please answer questions 3-5; otherwise go directly to question 6.

3) What do you like most about GIRL TALK books?

Check one: Characters_____ Situations_____
            Telephone Talk_____Other_____

4) Who is your favorite GIRL TALK character?

Check one: Sabrina_____ Katie_____ Randy_____
Allison_____ Stacy_____ Other (give name) _____

5) Who is your *least* favorite character?

_____

6) Where did you buy this GIRL TALK book?

Check one: Bookstore____Toy store____Discount store____
Grocery store___Supermarket___Other (give name)_____

Please turn over to continue survey.

7) How many GIRL TALK books have you read?
Check one: 0_____   1 to 2_____   3 to 4 _____   5 or more_____

8) In what type of store would you look for GIRL TALK books?
Bookstore_____Toy store_____Discount store_____
Grocery store_____Supermarket_____Other (give name)_____

9) Which type of store would you visit most often if you wanted to buy a GIRL TALK book?
Check *only* one: Bookstore_____Toy store_____
Discount store_____Grocery store_____Supermarket_____
Other (give name)_____

10) How many books do you read in a month?
Check one: 0_____   1 to 2_____   3 to 4 _____   5 or more_____

11) Do you read any of these books?
Check those you have read:
The Baby-sitters Club_____   Nancy Drew_____
Pen Pals_____   Sweet Valley High _____
Sweet Valley Twins_____Gymnasts_____

12) Where do you shop most often to buy these books?
Check one: Bookstore_____Toy store_____
Discount store_____Grocery store_____Supermarket_____
Other (give name)_____

13) What other kinds of books do you read most often?
_____

14) What would you like to read more about in GIRL TALK?
_____
_____

Send completed form to :
GIRL TALK Survey, Western Publishing Company, Inc.
1220 Mound Avenue, Mail Station #85
Racine, Wisconsin 53404

**LOOK FOR THE AWESOME GIRL TALK BOOKS IN
A STORE NEAR YOU!**

Fiction
#1 WELCOME TO JUNIOR HIGH!
#2 FACE-OFF!
#3 THE NEW YOU
#4 REBEL, REBEL
#5 IT'S ALL IN THE STARS
#6 THE GHOST OF EAGLE MOUNTAIN
#7 ODD COUPLE
#8 STEALING THE SHOW
#9 PEER PRESSURE
#10 FALLING IN LIKE
#11 MIXED FEELINGS
#12 DRUMMER GIRL
#13 THE WINNING TEAM
#14 EARTH ALERT!
#15 ON THE AIR
#16 HERE COMES THE BRIDE
#17 STAR QUALITY
#18 KEEPING THE BEAT
#19 FAMILY AFFAIR
#20 ROCKIN' CLASS TRIP
#21 BABY TALK
#22 PROBLEM DAD
#23 HOUSE PARTY
#24 COUSINS
#25 HORSE FEVER
#26 BEAUTY QUEENS
#27 PERFECT MATCH
#28 CENTER STAGE
#29 FAMILY RULES
#30 THE BOOKSHOP MYSTERY
#31 IT'S A SCREAM!
#32 KATIE'S CLOSE CALL
#33 RANDY AND THE *PERFECT* BOY

MORE GIRL TALK TITLES TO LOOK FOR

#34 ALLISON, SHAPE UP!
#35 KATIE AND SABRINA'S BIG COMPETITION
#36 SABRINA AND THE CALF-RAISING DISASTER
#37 RANDY'S BIG DREAM
#38 ALLISON TO THE RESCUE!
#39 KATIE AND THE IMPOSSIBLE COUSINS
#40 SABRINA WINS BIG!
#41 RANDY AND THE GREAT CANOE RACE
#42 ALLISON'S BABY-SITTING ADVENTURE
#43 KATIE'S BEVERLY HILLS FRIEND
#44 RANDY'S BIG CHANCE
#45 SABRINA AND TOO MANY BOYS

Nonfiction
ASK ALLIE 101 answers to your questions about boys, friends, family, and school!

YOUR PERSONALITY QUIZ Fun, easy quizzes to help you discover the real you!

BOYTALK: HOW TO TALK TO YOUR FAVORITE GUY